Hercules Doesn't Pull Teeth

W9-DGA-074

There are more books about the Bailey School Kids!
Have you read these adventures?

Hercules Doesn't Pull Teeth

by **Debbie Dadey**
and
Marcia Thornton Jones

illustrated by **John Steven Gurney**

A
LITTLE APPLE
PAPERBACK

SCHOLASTIC INC.
New York   Toronto   London   Auckland   Sydney

ISBN 0-590-25809-5

12 11 10 9 8 7 6 5 4 3 2 1   8 9/9 0 1/0 2/0 3/0

Printed in the U.S.A.   40

First Scholastic printing, March 1998

Book design by Laurie Williams

Contents

1

Dr. Zeus

"What kind of dumb name is that?" Eddie asked. "It sounds like a disease."

"It's my dentist's name," Liza explained as she pointed to the building directory. "Dr. Zeus has always been my dentist. He's very old and very nice." Eddie, Liza, and their friends Melody and Howie got on the elevator to go up to the twelfth floor. Liza had an after-school appointment with the dentist and her friends were coming with her.

"There's no such thing as a nice dentist," Eddie muttered, pulling off his baseball cap. "All they want to do is poke your gums until they bleed."

"That's not true," Liza said. "Dr. Zeus is very gentle."

Howie pushed button number twelve

1

on the elevator. "Zeus is a very famous name," he told Eddie.

"I know," Melody said. "It's from ancient Greece. There are stories about Zeus as a mighty god."

Eddie looked at Melody like she had sprouted carrots out her ears. "How did you know that?" Eddie asked.

Melody put her hands on her hips and tossed her black braids behind her shoulders. "I know lots of stuff. Zeus was the most important of the Greek gods. He's on a trading card I have at home. I have one for Zeus, another one for this creature called Medusa that has snakes on her head, and another one —"

"I think you have rocks in your head," Eddie joked. "Who cares about some dead guy that lived zillions of years ago?"

Melody shrugged. "Some of the stories on the back of the cards are neat."

The door to the elevator opened and the four kids walked into room 1212.

Thick purple carpets covered the floor and big gold chairs lined the walls. Heavy purple curtains were pulled back from the window with giant gold chains. "Wow," Eddie said. "This guy must be super rich. His office looks like a palace. Maybe I should be a dentist when I grow up."

Howie smiled. "I could be a doctor right next door to you." Howie had wanted to be a doctor since he'd been in kindergarten.

Eddie stabbed a finger toward Liza's mouth. "I could jab you in the jaw and you'd pay me money for it."

Liza shook her head. "Every other dentist would have to be dead before I'd let you put one grubby paw in my mouth."

"You'd better tell the receptionist you're here," Melody told Liza. Liza nodded and walked up to a window inside the waiting room. When Liza returned she was pale.

"What's wrong?" Melody asked.

"You look like someone ate your tongue," Eddie joked.

Liza looked like she was about to cry. "The most horrible thing in the world has happened!"

2

Lucky Twelve

"The television station broke down?" Eddie asked.

"I'm serious," Liza said.

"So am I," Eddie told her. "No television is the most horrible thing I can think of."

Howie patted Liza on the shoulder "What's wrong? Did the dentist cancel your appointment?"

Liza shook her head. "Worse," she said. "Dr. Zeus is missing."

"MISSING!" Melody shrieked. "Have the police been called?"

"Maybe they should hire a private detective," Eddie suggested. "They could use bloodhounds to sniff out his trail."

"They only use bloodhounds to sniff

out escaped criminals," Howie pointed out.

"People who pull teeth and drill holes in them sound like criminals to me," Eddie said matter-of-factly.

Howie was ready to argue with Eddie, but Liza interrupted. "Dr. Zeus is not a criminal. He's the best dentist in the world. Or at least he was until last week," Liza said sadly. "He retired and flew someplace sunny."

Eddie put his hands on his hips. "You told us he was missing!" Eddie said. "All he did was quit! What's wrong with that?"

"Now I have to see the new dentist," Liza said. She still looked ready to cry.

Melody shrugged. "I'm sure Dr. Zeus was careful about picking his replacement."

Liza sniffed and nodded. "The nurse told me the new dentist is his son. The receptionist said he would see me in twelve minutes."

"Twelve?" Howie asked. "That's weird."

"It looks like the new tooth dude in town likes the number twelve," Eddie said, pointing to the waiting room.

Melody, Liza, and Howie counted. "Twelve gold chairs," Howie said.

"There are twelve pictures on the wall, too," Melody said.

"That's strange," Howie said.

Eddie rolled his eyes. "If you ask me, twelve is better than unlucky thirteen!"

"Eddie's right," Melody said. "There is nothing to worry about."

Just then, a door squeaked open. "I am ready to see you now," a deep voice rumbled.

When the four kids turned around, they found themselves facing a giant.

3

Dr. Herb

The man was so tall he had to duck to get through the door. It only took him three steps to reach the kids. He towered over them and held out his hand.

"I am Dr. Herb," he said. "Your new dentist."

Liza's hand looked tiny when she shook Dr. Herb's hand. "I'm pleased to meet you," she said, but her voice shook.

Dr. Herb smiled. "No need to be scared," he said. "My father taught me everything he knew."

A super-sized white dentist's jacket covered Dr. Herb's watermelon-sized muscles. Right over his bulging chest muscles on the left side was a badge showing a picture of Earth. Purple letters

on the badge said: CHAMPION OF THE WORLD.

"I thought Atlas was the champion," Melody said. She remembered the legend of a strong man named Atlas who held up the world.

"Don't you know anything?" Eddie said. "An atlas is a book with maps in it."

Dr. Herb laughed so loud the glass in the door rattled. "Atlas needs no maps. He won't be going anywhere for a long, long time. But you," he said, pointing to Liza, "need to be going to room twelve so I can shine your teeth!"

Liza took a deep breath. "I'll be out soon," she told her friends.

Eddie nodded. "This guy will be quick. After all, he's so strong, he could pull a tooth with one flick of his pinkie."

Liza's hands flew to her mouth. "I don't need any teeth pulled," she mumbled through her fingers.

"You look as scared as my puppy did last summer," Dr. Herb said with a laugh.

"Boy, was he hot under his collar when I caught him. But I brought him home and now he's as lazy as a grizzly bear in winter."

Howie stood up tall. "I saved a homeless puppy, too," he said.

"Well," Dr. Herb said with a laugh. "My dog, Cerb, is happy to live with me, just as I'm sure Liza will be happy to have her teeth sparkling white." Dr. Herb held up ten fingers. Then he flashed two fingers. "She'll be out in twelve minutes," he said.

And then Dr. Herb and Liza disappeared through the door.

4

Cerb

"Do you think she'll be okay?" Melody asked. "Dr. Herb is the biggest dentist I've ever seen."

"He's the professional wrestler of the teeth-pulling world," Eddie agreed.

"I'm sure she'll be fine," Howie assured Melody.

"She's not having brain surgery," Eddie said. "She's only getting her teeth cleaned. Why don't we go play soccer while she's in there?"

Howie shook his head. "Dr. Herb said she'd only be twelve minutes. We wouldn't even have time to get downstairs from the twelfth floor before she was done."

"Dr. Herb sure likes the number twelve," Melody said. "If you ask me, it's a little strange."

Eddie stared at a picture on the wall. "This dog is a little strange, if you ask me." Howie and Melody looked at the picture, too. A huge brown dog with yellow eyes stared back at them. A gold plate under the picture had four letters: CERB.

"That's a weird name for a dog," Howie said.

Melody looked around the room and gulped. She pointed to two more pictures of huge dogs. Both dogs were brown and ferocious looking. Underneath each picture were the letters: CERB.

"It looks like an ugly dog convention to me," Eddie joked.

"Don't you think it's pretty strange that Dr. Herb has three dogs named Cerb?" Melody asked.

"Maybe he likes rhyming names," Howie suggested. "Cerb rhymes with Herb."

"Maybe he's lazy," Eddie said. "He could call all three dogs just by yelling Cerb once."

Melody looked around the room at the heavy purple drapes and the thick gold chains pulling them back. "Isn't purple a royal color?" she asked.

Howie nodded. "Kings and queens in the olden days wore purple for big ceremonies. No one else was allowed to wear purple."

"This place is giving me the creeps," Melody said. "I'm getting worried about Liza. I better check on her."

Howie looked at his watch. "I don't think it's been twelve minutes yet."

Melody didn't stop to think about the time. She just barged into room twelve and came face-to-face with a three-headed dog.

5

Greek Gods

"You didn't have to scream your head off," Liza told Melody after leaving the dentist's office. The kids were in the elevator going down from the twelfth floor. "It was only a statue of a dog."

Melody pushed her black braids out of her face and shrugged. "It surprised me, that's all."

"Why did you come into the examining room in the first place?" Liza asked. "I was almost done. Dr. Herb must have a magic toothbrush. I've never had my teeth cleaned so fast."

Eddie bopped Melody on the head with his baseball cap. "Melody was worried that King Kong dentist would carry you off to the Empire State Building," he told Liza.

19

"You have to admit, Dr. Herb is different from most dentists," Melody said.

"Nothing is wrong with being different," Liza pointed out.

The four kids stepped off the elevator and Melody pulled them close. "There is nothing wrong with being different, but there is something wrong with keeping a three-headed dog prisoner," she told her friends.

"What are you talking about?" Howie asked.

Eddie shook his head. "She's flipped out. She's lost her marbles. She's living in la-la land."

Melody put her hands on her hips. "I'm perfectly fine. Come to my house and I'll show you what I'm talking about."

"I want to play soccer," Eddie complained.

"I do, too," Melody told him. "But this is important."

"So is soccer," Eddie told her, but he trudged alongside his friends to Melody's house. In her room, Melody pulled out a big box of trading cards from under her bed.

Eddie's eyes lit up. "Now you're talking. I'll go home and get my baseball cards and we can trade."

"No," Melody said. "These aren't to trade. Just look." Melody spread purple and gold cards out on her floor. Across the top of each card were gold letters that said: GREEK GODS AND GODDESSES. Every card had a different picture. There

was one of a strong man holding a lightning bolt. Purple letters at the bottom named him ZEUS.

Liza pointed at the name Zeus. "Hey, that's my old dentist's name."

Melody pointed to another card. It had a young man with bulging muscles carrying a lion on his shoulder.

"Big deal," Eddie said. "He has muscles, but what's his batting average?"

"They didn't have baseball back in those days," Howie explained. "That's Hercules. He was the strongest man in the world."

Melody nodded. "He had to perform twelve superhuman labors in twelve years. He did things no ordinary human could do."

"If he was so great, he should have played sports," Eddie said. "Then he could have been really famous."

Liza picked up the card. "Hercules *is* famous. But I don't understand why you wanted to show us these cards."

"Because," Melody said slowly, "I think Dr. Herb is . . ."

"Is who?" Eddie asked impatiently.

Melody grabbed the card from Liza. "Dr. Herb is Hercules!"

24

6

Underworld Pets

Howie and Liza giggled, but Eddie laughed right out loud. He laughed so hard he rolled on the floor, grabbing a handful of Melody's trading cards and throwing them high in the air. One of the cards floated down and bopped Howie on top of his head.

Howie stopped laughing when he saw the picture on the card.

"Hey," Howie shouted.

Eddie, Liza, and Melody all froze and stared at their friend. "What's wrong?" Liza asked. "You look like you just found out you need four teeth pulled!"

"That wouldn't bother me," Howie said, "as long as I knew the dentist didn't get his pets in the underworld."

"Most pets don't live underwater," Eddie said.

"I'm not talking about water," Howie said. "I'm talking about the evil underworld."

"You must mean under Eddie's bed," Liza said with a giggle.

"No," Melody said. "Hercules captured the three-headed dog that guarded the underworld. It was the last of his twelve challenges."

"Big deal," Eddie said. "Hercules probably left a trail of doggy treats. Even I could figure that out and I'm not Hercules."

"I hope you're right," Howie said. "But then, how do you explain this?"

Howie tossed the card on the floor in front of his friends. It landed faceup, showing a picture of a mean-looking dog with three heads. "Look close," Howie told his friends. Liza, Melody, and Eddie bent low over the picture.

"Its name is Cerberus," Howie pointed out.

"My name is Eddie," Eddie said. "And your name must be Larry Lunatic."

Liza nodded. "You sound as crazy as Melody."

"I'm not crazy!" Melody said. "Dr. Herb is very strange."

"She's right," Howie said. "Liza's dentist has three pictures of dogs named Cerb that look just like the monster dog on this trading card. I think Cerb is short for Cerberus!"

Melody clapped her hands. "I bet after Hercules got back from the underworld everybody was afraid of the three-headed dog so he decided to keep it as a pet. The pictures in his office are of Cerberus!"

"Dr. Herb is not keeping a three-headed monster as a pet," Eddie said. "He just has three different dogs with the same name."

"Exactly," Liza said. "Just like there have been lots of dogs named Lassie."

Howie shook his head. "There's something fishy about Dr. Herb," he said. "We have to get to the bottom of it!"

7

The Weight of the Sky

"It's all your fault," Melody snapped.

Liza shrugged. "I didn't do anything," she said.

"Yes, you did," Melody argued. "You told my mom about Dr. Herb and that reminded her that I haven't been to a dentist in a long time. Now I have to go to Dr. Herb, and I bet he finds a cavity." Melody held her hand to her cheek and moaned.

Melody and her three friends met in their favorite place, under the giant oak tree on the Bailey School playground. They were supposed to play soccer, but Melody had to go to the dentist instead.

"Do you have a toothache?" Howie asked.

"No," Melody said. "But I bet I will after Dr. Herb is finished with me."

"The worst part," Eddie said, "is that you'll be sitting in a stuffy dentist's office instead of playing soccer."

"No fair," Melody cried. "You went to the dentist with Liza. Now you should go with me. We can play when I get finished with the dentist."

"Oh, no," Eddie said, backing away from Melody. "I'm not hanging around a tooth driller's torture chamber again when I could be playing soccer!"

"Wait," Howie said. "Melody has a point."

"So does the dentist," Eddie said. "And it drills right down into raw nerves."

Melody screamed and covered her mouth with her hands.

"Stop it," Liza said. "Dr. Herb won't hurt Melody. And it won't hurt us to go with her."

"Aw, shucks," Eddie said, kicking at the

trunk of the oak tree. "There goes my soccer game."

"It'll be worth it," Liza said, "when you see Melody's sparkling smile."

Eddie grumbled all the way to the dentist, but his three friends ignored him. They rode the elevator to the twelfth floor and settled into the chairs in office 1212. In twelve minutes, Dr. Herb beamed at them and Melody disappeared down the hallway to get her teeth cleaned.

Melody scooted past the statue of Cerberus and settled into the dentist's chair. "You look very tired," Melody said when Dr. Herb stretched his back.

"It has been a busy week," Dr. Herb said. "You're my tenth patient and my back is killing me. I feel like I've been holding up the weight of the sky."

"That would make you Atlas," Melody said.

Dr. Herb frowned. "That Atlas, he al-

ways gets the credit," Dr. Herb growled. "He never admits he had help!"

Melody gulped. "I didn't mean to make you mad," she said.

Dr. Herb shrugged. "I'm not angry at you," he said. "But I've been on many journeys and it's the same wherever I go. The wrong person gets all the credit."

"That's not always true," Melody said. "When people work hard they get credit in Bailey City."

"Exactly!" Dr. Herb said and pounded his fist on the counter. When he did, the toothbrush he was holding snapped in two. "That's why I came here. I plan to clean out Bailey City!"

Melody whimpered. "Clean out?"

Dr. Herb looked at Melody and smiled. "I'm talking about teeth!" he said. "My challenge is to check every tooth in Bailey City. And you're next on the list!"

And then Dr. Herb came straight at Melody.

8

Superhuman Muscle Men

When Melody ran down the hallway and burst into the waiting room, her friends jumped up. "What's wrong?" Liza asked. "Do you have a cavity?"

Melody glanced over her shoulder and moaned. She grabbed Howie's and Liza's arms and pulled them out the door of office 1212. Eddie followed close behind.

"Do you have to get braces?" Eddie asked.

Melody shook her head, but she didn't answer until they were safely on the elevator. "I wish it was just a cavity or braces," Melody said.

"Going to the dentist isn't as fun as playing soccer," Liza admitted. "But it's nothing to be so scared about."

"It *is* scary when the dentist is Hercules," Melody said as they left the office building. "And he's planning on taking over Bailey City."

"Not that strongman story again," Eddie complained. "I'm pretty sure Dr. Herb is not Hercules," he said. "After all, Hercules doesn't pull teeth."

Liza giggled. "Eddie's right. Hercules is a made-up story. There are no such things as superhuman muscle men and dogs with three heads."

"But he told me he was here on a challenge," Melody argued. "A challenge is just like the labors Hercules had to complete."

"Did he really say he was going to take over Bailey City?" Howie asked.

Melody pulled her friends into the shadow of a nearby building. "I figured out he plans to crush the other dentists in town," Melody whispered. "It's up to us to stop him!"

"This is worse than I thought," Eddie said.

"Then you believe Melody?" Liza asked.

"No," Eddie said. "This is worse because Melody is beyond crazy. Her brain has turned into toothpaste!"

"If you're so sure Dr. Herb is a normal dentist," Howie said slowly, "then you won't be scared to prove it."

"The only thing I'm scared of is Melody's brains oozing out her ears," Eddie said.

"Okay," Howie said. "Then I have a plan. We'll follow Dr. Herb home."

"What will that prove?" Liza asked.

Melody grabbed Liza's arm. "I know," Melody whispered. "If we find out where Dr. Herb lives, we'll see his three-headed dog."

"There is no three-headed monster dog," Liza said, "except in your imagination."

"Then you'll go?" Howie asked.

"I'll do anything," Eddie said, "to get you to stop talking this Hercules nonsense."

Howie and Melody nodded. "We'll meet here," Melody said, "just as the sun is setting."

"Fine," Eddie said. "I'll be ready."

"Ready to fight Hercules?" Liza asked.

"No," Eddie said. "Ready to prove Melody and Howie are wrong!"